'Sonny the Sea Tractor'
is an original concept by Loretta D'Souza
© Loretta D'Souza 2010

Author Loretta D'Souza
Illustrated by Ewa Poklewska
Ewa Poklewska is represented by MSM Studio
www.msmstudio.eu

Maverick Arts Publishing Ltd
Studio 4, Hardham Mill Park
Pulborough
West Sussex RH20 1LA
+44 (0) 179887 5980

© Maverick Arts Publishing Limited (2010)

**PUBLISHED BY MAVERICK ARTS
PUBLISHING LTD**

ISBN 978-1-84886-036-0

Maverick
arts publishing
www.maverickartsclub.com

SONNY

by Loretta D'Souza

Illustrated by Ewa Poklewska

It's a sunny afternoon at Koob Beach.
Netty and Harry are building a sandcastle.

"I'm bored," says Netty.
"Shall we play hide and seek?"

"Yes......I'll count to 20
and then look for you."

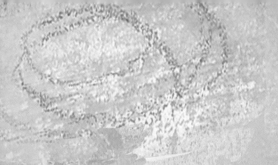

"Ok," Netty runs off
and Harry begins to count to Twenty!

"One, two, three, four, five, six, seven, eight, nine, ten......twenty.

I'm coming!"

"Where is she?"

Harry runs towards the rocks, but she's not there.

Harry notices an old shed.

"Aha that's where she'll be!"

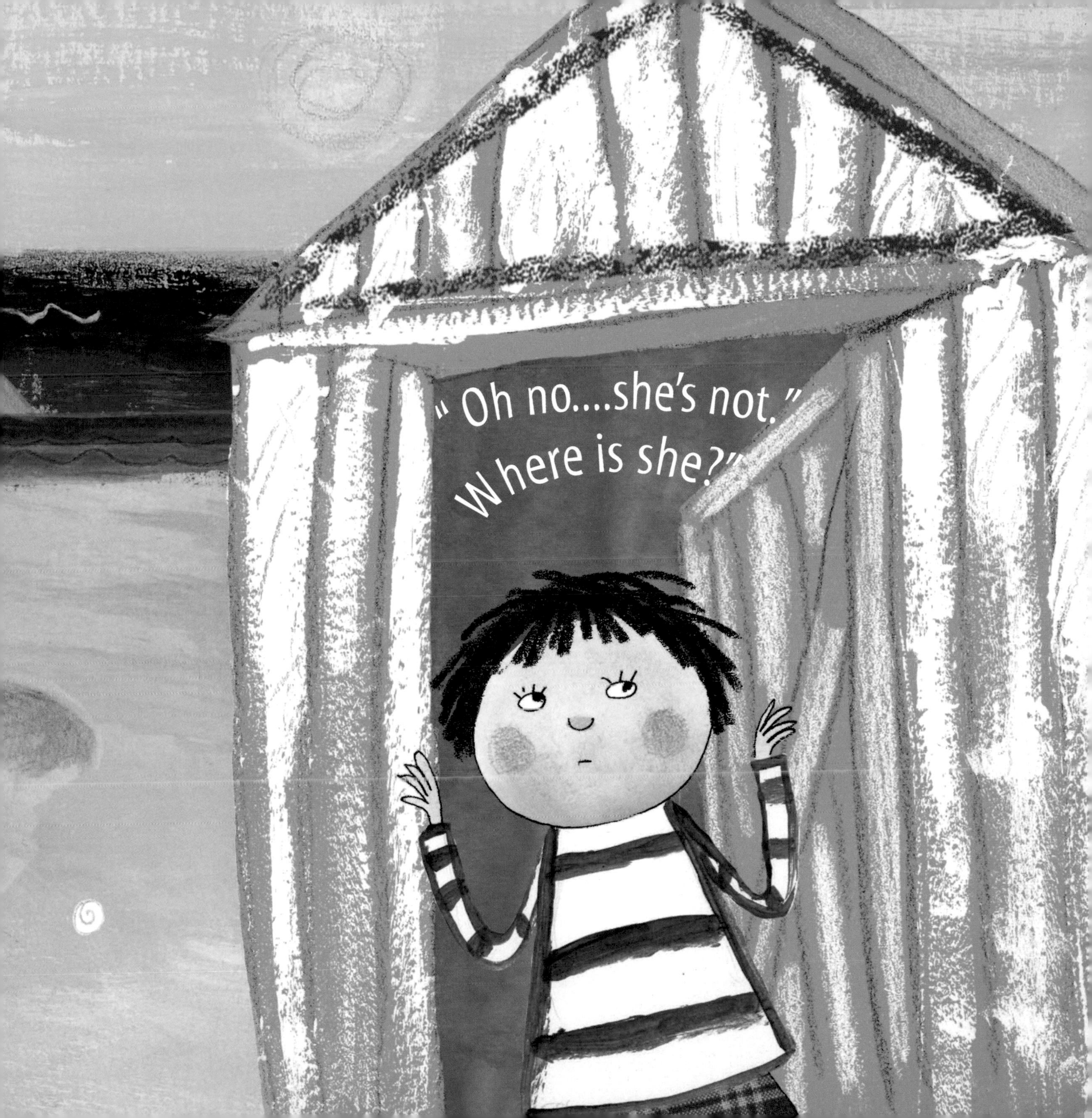

" Oh no....she's not."
"Where is she?"

"We know where she is," chirps Stephen Seagull.

"Where?" asks Harry.

"What will you give us if we tell you?"

"I haven't got anything to give you," says Harry.

"That's a shame, we won't tell you where she is then," chirps in Molly.

"Please tell me,
it's getting late and we need
to be going home," begs Harry.

And then suddenly...

"Help!! Help me! I'm stuck."

"Netty! Where are you?" shouts Harry.

Stephen Seagull and Molly panic.
They get into a flap and start squawking.

"Follow us," says Stephen Seagull.

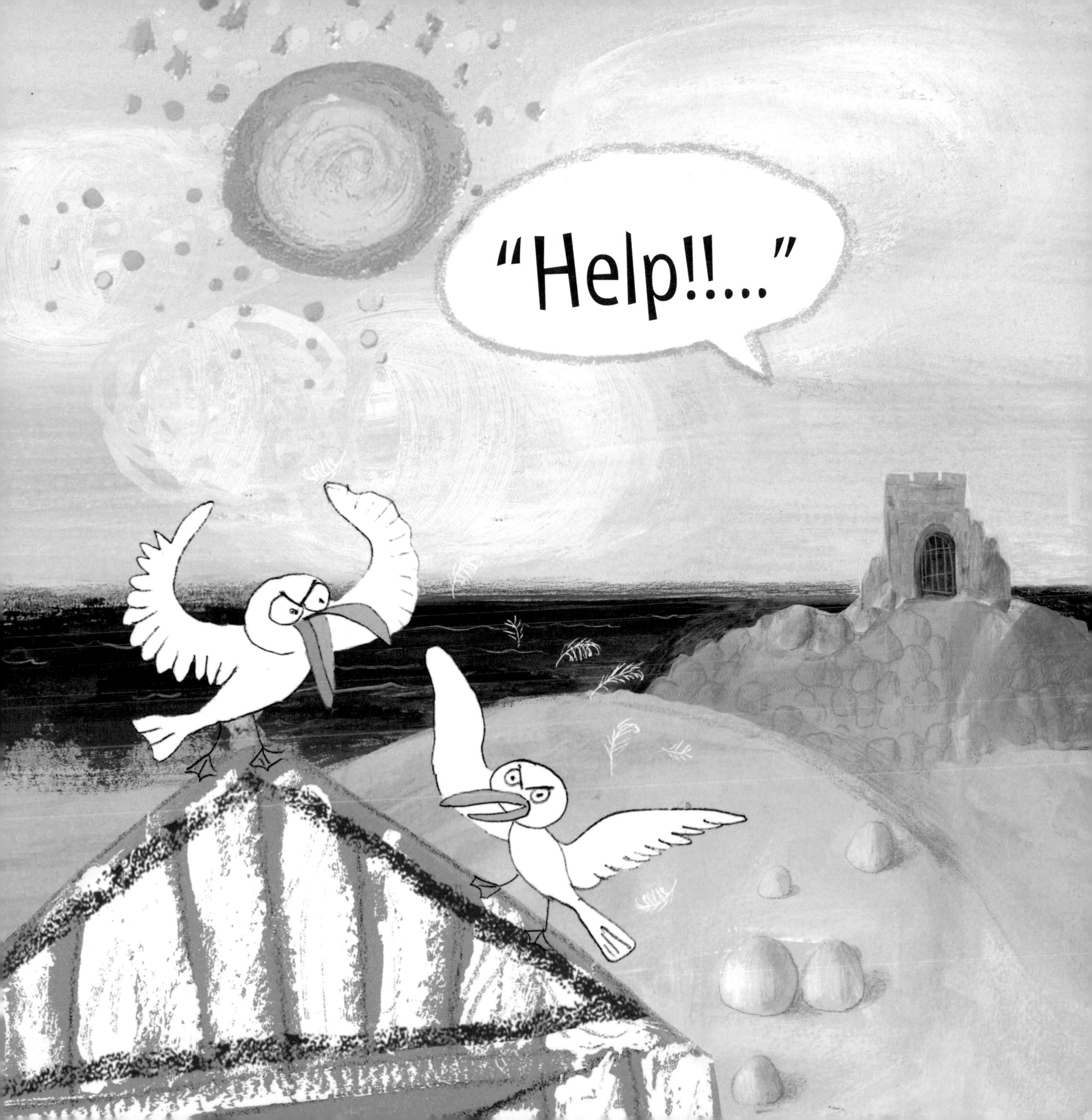
"Help!!..."

The castle on Koob Island,
is beginning to get cut off from the
main beach because the tide is coming in.

"Heeeellllllp." yells Netty.

"We're coming....
"we're coming!" shouts Harry.

"It's stuck! ...it won't open."

The tide is coming in fast.

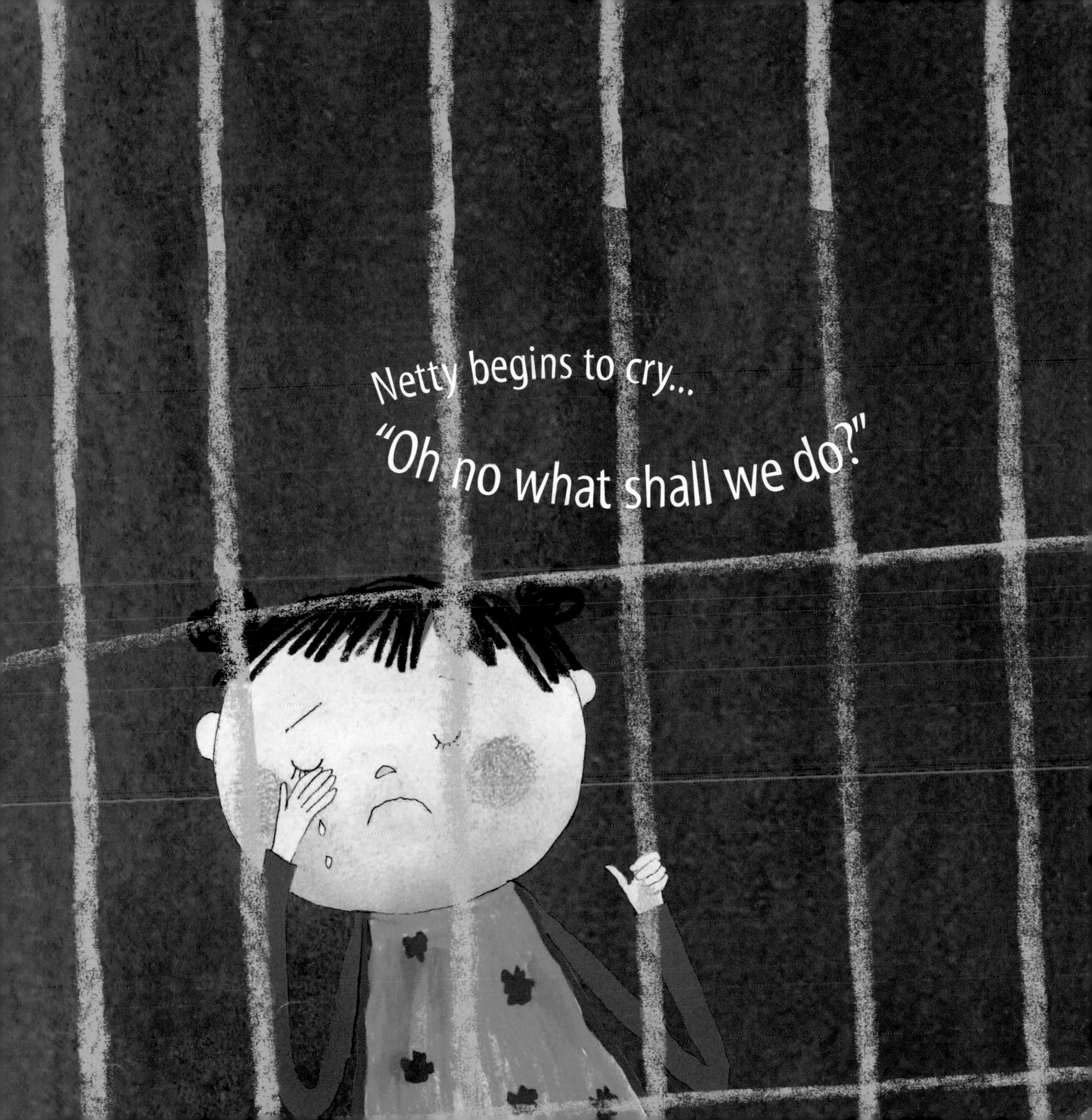

Netty begins to cry...

"Oh no what shall we do?"

"Don't worry...Sonny will help. "
squawks Molly.

Like lightning the two seagulls soar up
into the sky, as high as the clouds.

Meanwhile Stephen Seagull and
Molly find Sonny the Sea Tractor
and tell him whats going on...

When Sonny gets to the Island, Scampi the fat sea cat leaps off his roof and scrambles up the rocks with a rope in his teeth.

"Hurry.. Hurry... Hurry." yell Harry and Netty.

"Don't worry kids, we'll save you,"

says Scampi,

as he ties the rope around the iron gate.

"Ok Sonny, it's tied on," yells Scampi.

Sonny tries to pull the gate away
from the castle....

Nothing happens! Sonny revs the engine and pulls even harder.
At last the gate gives way and Netty is free!

"You're safe now," says Scampi.

"Come on let's get you home."

"Netty was lucky **we** were there to help!"

"You shouldn't be playing there,
its too easy to get stranded!" says Sonny.

"We certainly won't be
playing there again!"

says Netty relieved.

"Remember the tide is high twice a day.
Never go off by yourselves and
always play where there are a lot of people about."

"Is it your job to save kids like us?"
asks Netty thankfully.

"Not really...but I'm always here when anyone needs me."
says Sonny as he carries Harry and Netty to safety.

"So what treats are you going to give us for helping you?"

asks Stephen Seagull.

"Treats?" exclaims Harry.

"You naughty seagulls didn't want to help in the first place!"

"I should get Scampi to eat you both for breakfast!"

...They all start laughing

Sonny the Sea Tractor brings Harry and Netty safely
back to the main beach.

"Thanks Sonny... We'll tell everyone how you saved us!"

The End.